Beaver
Gets Lost

A Little Animal Adventure

Beaver Gets Lost

Written by Ariane Chottin
Adapted by Deborah Kovacs
Illustrations by Marcelle Geneste

Published by The Reader's Digest Association Limited
London ❖ New York ❖ Sydney ❖ Montreal

Once upon a time a family of red
squirrels lived among the oak trees in a little
wood beside a bubbling stream. One crisp
autumn day as the young squirrels played on
a hollow log, a funny little animal with dark
brown fur waddled up.

'I think I'm lost,' he said.

'Don't worry,' said Mother Squirrel.
'We'll take care of you.'

The little squirrel children were delighted.

'Hooray! We've got a new brother to play with,' they cried.

'My name is Josie,' said one little squirrel, scrambling down the tree trunk. 'What's yours?'

'Clarence,' said the little animal shyly.

Clarence soon settled into squirrel family life and his new brothers and sisters were delighted with their playmate. As far as they were concerned, he was one of them. But one thing puzzled Father Squirrel and that was Clarence's unusual tail. It was flat and covered with black scales, not fluffy and red like his tail and the tails of all the other family members.

One day, Father Squirrel tried to
teach the children how to build a nest. But
the young squirrels wouldn't sit still for the
lesson. They chased each other up trees
and tossed acorns from the branches. Only
Clarence paid attention. He listened very
carefully to every word that Father
Squirrel said.

'I can't wait to build my own nest!' said Clarence. He got straight to work, dragging long branches across the forest to the clearing.

As he worked, Clarence's nest began to look very different from the one Father Squirrel had built. Instead of piling up layers of leaves and twigs, Clarence took large sticks and stood them upright, leaning one against the other, then he used his tail to pat mud into the cracks.

Back and forth he went, dragging bigger and bigger branches past his astonished family.

For days, Clarence kept working.
Josie sat up on a branch and watched him.
She couldn't understand it. She wished he
would play with her instead.

'When will you finish building?' she
asked him.

Clarence looked at his nest. 'Not for a
long time,' he answered. 'There's still a lot
of work to do here.'

Clarence's building skills were the talk of the woods! Animals came from far and near to watch the crazy young squirrel with the strange tail.

'What is he doing?' asked a weasel.

'He's been building that thing for days,' said Josie. 'He never stops. Work, work, work all the time!'

Clarence's nest got bigger and bigger and still he kept on building.

'Do you want a hand?' Josie asked, hoping that she could help him to finish off his work.

'Oh, yes!' said Clarence. 'Would you please help me to find more branches to use while I cut down this tree?'

'OK,' sighed Josie, scampering off into the woods.

As she looked for branches by the river at the edge of the wood, Josie suddenly got the biggest surprise. There – in front of her eyes – was a whole family of animals just like Clarence! They had big front teeth and broad flat tails and they were building a huge nest of sticks.

'Gosh!', said Josie. 'Just wait till I tell everyone!'

Josie was quite out of breath after rushing back to the family oak tree in the middle of the forest.

'Clarence! Clarence!' she cried. 'There are lots of squirrels who look just like you and are making a nest just like yours, down on the river. I think I've found your family!'

'Where, Josie?' cried Clarence. 'Please show me!'

'May we come, too?' the young squirrels begged their parents.

'Why not?' said Mother Squirrel.

Everyone rushed after Josie and Clarence, who were heading for the riverbank.

There in a big stick hut that looked just like the nest that Clarence had built was a whole family of Clarences, big and small.

'Who are you?' asked Father Squirrel.

'We're beavers!' they chorused as Clarence raced to his mother's side.

'Thank you so much for looking after my son,' she said to Mother Squirrel. 'I thought I had lost him for ever!'

'That explains it,' said Father Squirrel. 'He was such an amazing builder for a squirrel and we did wonder about his tail!'

It was celebration time. Mother Beaver brought apples, mushrooms and acorns. The happy little animals had a feast.

Then Clarence plunged into the water for a long, refreshing swim.

All about ... **BEAVERS**

POWERFUL TEETH
The beaver belongs to a big family of animals known as rodents, who all have sharp front teeth. It is the biggest rodent in Europe. Others include squirrels, rats and mice.

FACT FILE
UNDERWATER EXPERTS
Beavers are superb swimmers. When they build their homes or need to hide, they can stay under water for 20 minutes without coming up for air.

MAKING A SPLASH
When a beaver senses danger, it slaps its heavy tail on the water, making a big splash. This warns all the other beavers to hide under water.

GETTING A LIFT

Beavers are good parents and stay together for life. They have two to four babies each year and look after them until they are two years old. When she swims, the mother beaver carries her little ones on her back or on her tail, or she may grip them with her teeth.

Did you know?

FEELING AT HOME

Beavers love building and create big barricades of sticks to fence off the water and create their own personal lake where they can swim and fish, and build their homes, known as 'lodges'.

MAKING A COMEBACK

Once upon a time there were beavers everywhere and there are still a lot of North American beavers. But in Europe, they were often hunted for their beautiful fur and are now much more rare, though in Scotland and elsewhere they are gradually being reintroduced.

YOUNG FAMILIES

Beaver Gets Lost is a Little Animal Adventures book
published by Reader's Digest Young Families, Inc.
by arrangement with Éditions Nathan, Paris, France

Written by Ariane Chottin
Adapted by Deborah Kovacs
Illustrations by Marcelle Geneste
Notebook artwork © Paul Bommer

This edition was adapted and published in 2007 by
The Reader's Digest Association Limited
11 Westferry Circus, Canary Wharf, London E14 4HE

We are committed to both the quality of our products
and the service we provide to our customers.
We value your comments, so please feel free to contact us on
08705 113366 or via our website at:
www.readersdigest.co.uk
If you have any comments or suggestions about the content of our books,
you can contact us at:
gbeditorial@readersdigest.co.uk

Printed in China.

Book code: 637-006 UP0000-1
ISBN: 978 0 276 44235 3
Oracle code: 501800026H.00.24